Scholastic's The Magic School Bus®

GETS EATEN

A Book About Food Chains

Scholastic Inc.

New York Toronto London Auckland Sydney

Based on the animated TV series
produced by Scholastic Productions, Inc.
Based on *The Magic School Bus* books
written by Joanna Cole and illustrated by Bruce Degen.

TV tie-in adaptation by Patricia Relf and illustrated by Carolyn Bracken
TV script written by John May and Jocelyn Stevenson

ISBN 0-590-48414-1

12 11 10 9 8 7 6 5 4 3 2 1   6 7 8 9/9 0 1/0

Printed in the U.S.A.   24

First Scholastic printing, January 1996

It was field trip day for our class. And a field trip with our teacher, Ms. Frizzle, is always ... well, an *experience*!

We were going to the beach. Ms. Frizzle had asked us to work in teams of two and to bring in beach things that go together.

Phoebe brought dune grass, and Ralphie brought a yellow balloon. "It's the sun," he said. "The sun makes the grass grow."

Wanda brought a mussel, and Tim brought a rock for it to live on.

But Keesha had forgotten about the beach things. "Oh, no! Oh, bad! Oh, bad, bad!" moaned Keesha. "All I brought was my beach towel and a tuna fish sandwich for lunch!"

AND the green slime on your shoes!

Just then, Arnold walked in. His shoes squeaked when he walked.

"Arnold! My *dear* partner!" said Keesha. "Did you by any chance bring *two* beach things that go together? I forgot about our report."

Arnold groaned. "Aargh! I forgot, too!" he said. "I was in such a hurry this morning that I ran all the way here and kind of stepped in the pond by our house. I didn't have time to change. So all I have is my bathing suit and a towel..."

Keesha and Arnold felt terrible. "How can we do our report?" said Arnold.

Keesha looked at her tuna fish sandwich. "We'll just have to work with what we have," she said. She looked at the green scum on Arnold's shoes. "There *must* be a way for a tuna sandwich and green scum to go together. Think!"

"Good morning, class!" Ms. Frizzle said. "Today is beach day. Let's hear some of your beach reports." She looked around the room.

Keesha and Arnold tried to look small.

"Keesha and Arnold!" Ms. Frizzle said brightly. "Tell us about your two beach things that go together."

Uh-oh!

I never thought I'd be glad to go on a field trip!

Saved by the beep!

Keesha stood up. "Well ... Arnold and I brought this nutritious tuna fish sandwich and ..." Keesha gulped. She grabbed Arnold's slimy shoe. "And this delightful green scum!" We all held our breaths, waiting to see what the Friz would say.

Ms. Frizzle smiled. "Fantastic!" she said. "Please go on! Tell us why a tuna sandwich and green scum belong —" A loud beep interrupted Ms. Frizzle. "Sorry! Hold that thought! It's time for our field trip."

We all piled onto the Magic School Bus and fastened our seat belts.

"Off we go!" said Ms. Frizzle. "Oh, I do like to be beside the seaside! I hope you all brought your bathing suits."

The Friz smiled. "The best way to learn about something is to jump right in," she said. "So hold on tightly, class!"

"Does that mean what I think it means?" asked Arnold.

I was afraid of this....

Suddenly the bus lurched toward the ocean.

Cool!

It flopped.   It flipped.

And then it jumped up and into the water, just like a dolphin.

Diving through the water, we could see seaweed all around us. "What are those beautiful, spiny rocks?" asked Tim.

"They're animals — sea urchins!" answered the Friz. "They eat seaweed." As we watched, a sea otter swam by and grabbed one of the sea urchins.

"And I guess otters eat the sea urchins," said Ralphie.

Do you think they *otter*?

"Otters eat urchins, urchins eat seaweed," said Ms. Frizzle. "See the connections?"

"I can't see anything through this green stuff," said Keesha. "It's all scummy out there."

"Did you say *scummy*?" Arnold asked. "That's it! Look, Keesha! Scum!"

Ms. Frizzle looked pleased. "Shall we take a closer look?" she asked.

Ms. Frizzle pressed a button, and, suddenly, we were shrinking. "There we go!" she said. "We are now as tiny as the green phytoplankton."

"That's *seriously* tiny!" whispered Tim.

"Class, please put on the specially designed underwater breathing masks that you will find under your seats. Then off we go! Remember, look for connections!" said the Friz as she opened the door of the bus.

"According to my research, phytoplankton live in the part of the ocean near the surface that gets sunlight," explained Dorothy Ann.

"Look at me!" said Dorothy Ann as she rode on one of the phytoplankton. Just then, a much bigger creature floated by and ate the phytoplankton out from under her. "Yikes!" she yelled. "Look out, everyone! We're the right size to be some-body's food."

HELP!

Just in time, the Magic School Bus swam by and grabbed us in a net. "All aboard," called Ms. Frizzle. "As I always say, it's better to be in the bus than in someone else!"

"Quick, let's get big!" begged Arnold.

"No sooner said than done," answered Ms. Frizzle. And with a spin and a *whoosh*, we grew to the size of the thing that had just tried to eat us. Ms. Frizzle said it is called zooplankton.

"Whew! We're safe!" said Arnold.

We looked out at the strange creatures floating around us. "Look at these guys," said Carlos.

"They are not 'guys,' they're zooplankton," said Wanda. "But what is that huge thing?" she asked, pointing to a fish that looked enormous to us.

"That is an anchovy, Wanda," said Ms. Frizzle.
Ralphie shuddered. His dad ate salty anchovies on pizza.
Now that yucky fish wanted to eat him!

Ms. Frizzle pressed a yellow button, and we felt ourselves growing again. In a few seconds, we were as big as the anchovies.

Ms. Frizzle said, "I suggest we stay on the bus while we have our lunch."

Keesha took out her tuna sandwich.

"Don't eat our report!" said Arnold. "Here, have a potato chip."

Keesha looked at her sandwich. "I still don't get it. How is this sandwich connected with your scum, Arnold?" she asked.

Arnold shrugged. "Tuna fish is just tuna fish," he said.

Keesha looked amazed. "Brilliant, Arnold!" she said. "Get it? It's like a chain. The scum is phytoplankton. Phytoplankton are eaten by zooplankton. Zooplankton are eaten by anchovies. And anchovies are eaten by *bigger* fish like —"

"TUNA!" yelled Arnold, looking out the window.

Suddenly, everything went dark. The bus bounced against something and came to a stop. "Where are we?" someone yelled.

Ms. Frizzle turned on the lights. "Class," she announced, "we are now inside an albacore tuna."

Keesha was excited. "This is great, Arnold!" she said. "Now we know how your green scum is connected to my sandwich!"

Keesha raised her hand. "Ms. Frizzle!" she called. "May we go back to school now? Arnold and I are ready to give our report!"

Ms. Frizzle smiled. "Certainly! Hold still, everyone. Here comes our chance!"

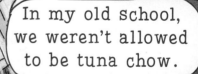
In my old school, we weren't allowed to be tuna chow.

At last we could see daylight. The bus was in the tuna's mouth … and the tuna's mouth was headed for a fishhook! "Seat belts, please," called Ms. Frizzle, and she pulled a lever. A clamp shot out from the Magic School Bus and fastened us onto the fishhook. We were caught! We flew through the air as someone reeled us in.

Yikes! I can't look!

A huge face peered at us as we dangled from the fishing line. "Another school bus!" the fisherwoman said thoughtfully. "Second one today. Back it goes!" She unhooked the bus and tossed us back into the ocean.

"We're a keeper!" yelled Arnold, but it was too late. The bus landed back in the water with a splash.

"Never fear, Arnold," said the Friz as she pressed another button on the dashboard.

"When in the surf, do as the surfers do!" Ms. Frizzle yelled over the sound of the waves. And before we knew it, we were surfing back to shore on the back of the Magic School Bus.

Back at school, Arnold and Keesha finally gave their report. "It's like a chain, with everything connected," said Arnold. "Tiny plants — like the scum on my shoe — are eaten by zooplankton. The zooplankton are eaten by anchovies."

"The anchovies are eaten by tuna fish," continued Keesha. "And, last of all, the tuna fish is eaten by ME! I guess that puts me at the top of *this* food chain, and am I ever hungry!"

"*Excellent* report on an ocean food chain!" exclaimed Ms. Frizzle. "What about a land food chain?"

"Well, a mouse eats grass seed," said Tim. "Then a snake might eat the mouse."

"And a hawk eats the snake!" finished Wanda. "The hawk is at the top of *that* food chain."

"Correct!" said Ms. Frizzle as she drew on the board. "And plants are at the bottom of almost every food chain."

It was time to go home. Arnold put on his scummy shoe. "Nature amazes me," he said.

"So does Ms. Frizzle!" said Keesha, and we all laughed — even Ms. Frizzle.

Dear Editor:

As a writer for *Fish Time* magazine, I want to inform you that tuna fish do not eat people or buses. They eat small fish such as anchovies.

Fondly,
In the Swim

Dear Editor:

My school bus cannot turn into a dolphin or anchovy or zoo-plankton. Our bus has trouble just turning into our street!

Signed,
The Bus Stops Here

Dear Editor:

Please let Arnold know that it is important to do homework on time, to remember to take it to school with you, and to keep your sneakers clean at all times.

From,
Tie Your Shoes

A Note to Teachers and Parents

When the Magic School Bus is eaten by a tuna, it becomes part of a food chain — a series of living things dependent upon one another for food.

Plants, which create food using energy from the sun, are at the bottom of almost every food chain. Herbivores eat plants, and carnivores eat herbivores.

Humans are at the top of many food chains. Encourage children to think about the food chains to which they belong and about how living things depend on one another.

Ms. Frizzle